The Snarls

A Hair Combing Story

Becca Price

[signature]

Interior art by Tanya Gleadall

Contents

The Snarls

Deep in the heart of pillows, or blown on the wind live the Snarls. Together with their cousins the Tangles, they wait, watching... searching for a child with long, fine hair, or very curly hair, and a place to build their homes.

The Tangles are mostly gentle folk, who go ranging to find homes for them all. If they find short hair, the Tangles make camp, but don't plan to settle. With short hair, there's really no place for the Tangles to hide.. They flee when they hear the crackle of a brush, or feel the bite of a comb.

But the Snarls are a different folk entirely.

Once a Tangle reports back to the Snarls that there's long hair ahead or fine hair or curly hair, or hair that badly needs washing, the Snarls move in.

First they build homesteads; small nests made of hair and dirt. But they quickly outgrow their little homes, because the Snarls multiply quickly. Soon the nests are full to overflowing with Snarl mothers and fathers, baby Snarls, toddler Snarls, preschool Snarls and kindergarten Snarls. Soon there are Grader Snarls, and teenager Snarls, and all their friends. The nest gets so crowded that there's no room for any more Snarls. So they have to build a bigger nest.

The bigger nest is full of sister and brother Snarls, aunt and uncle Snarls, and cousin Snarls. With all those children, they need to build Snarl schools, and so soon there are teacher Snarls and principal Snarls, and the schools are full of Snarl desks and Snarl books and Snarl crayons and Snarl playgrounds.

Well! Schools attract other Snarls, and soon there are dozens of Snarl nests – practically a whole village of them! And the Snarls need roads to get from their homes to the school, and they need Snarl food to eat and Snarl clothes to wear. So they build roads, and shops and plant gardens. And then they build even more nests, so that the villages grow into whole towns and cities!

Snarl towns and Snarl cities need even more roads to connect them, so that the Snarls can visit their friends and family and relatives. Soon the gardens can't grow enough food for all those Snarls, so they plant farms and build Snarl factories to make Snarl furniture and Snarl stoves and even Snarl refrigerators. Eventually, with all the visiting back and forth, and all the goods being shipped from one place to another, the Snarl roads develop Snarl traffic jams.

So, the Snarls build Snarl harbors and Snarl train stations, and lay Snarl train tracks everywhere. And when the Snarl ships and trains get too full, they build Snarl airplanes and airports, to carry Snarls from one place to another even faster.

And the more the Snarls travel, the more they build nests, and have baby Snarls, and build Snarl schools and Snarl farms and Snarl shops and Snarl grocery stores. But the one thing the Snarls *don't* build are barbershops!

For Snarls hate and fear barbers, and anyone who washes and cuts hair. Most of all, however, they hate and fear even more their natural enemies, the Combs and Brushes. Combs and Brushes chase the Snarls away, although they don't go without a fight. They pull and tug at the hair, until the unlucky owner cries from pain.

The Snarls can fight even Combs and Brushes, or could until someone invented anti-Snarl detangler. Mommies and Daddies use the dreaded detangler and Combs and Brushes and Water and Soap.

The first warning the Snarls have that they can't have their way anymore is when it starts to rain. Snarl nests and schools and roads and buildings and shops and airports are pretty strong, and can resist the rain when it's only Water. But then, to the rain is added Soap!

Great bubbles of Soap, washing away the dirt and grime that holds their buildings together! Mounds of Soap, like huge tidal waves, wash away the villages and towns and cities!

But Snarls are cunning builders and even Water and Soap, damaging though they may be, can't drive the Snarls away. Oh, some of the smaller Snarls get washed down the drain, but the huge Snarls fight back and cling to the hair even harder.

Then great lashings of Conditioner are added to the Water. Oh, how the Snarls despise Conditioner! It coats each hair with a thin film, so that the hair slides against the other hairs, rather than letting the hair cling to each other in the great Snarl nests. And Oh! the Water! Washing out the Soap, rinsing out the Conditioner, and taking with it all of the Snarl works.

But sometimes even Water and Soap and Conditioner aren't enough when the Snarls have really settled in. But then come the loving, patient – oh, ever so patient! – Mommies and Daddies with their dreaded weapons, the Comb and the Brush.

Oh, the crackle of the Brush, as the bristles move through the hair! The fierce bite of the Comb sends the Snarls running.

But not without a fight, oh no, not without a fight!

Snarl roads and train tracks and airports are built to last. The Snarls cling to the hair, and dig in their claws against the Brush and Comb. They fight inch, by inch, until at last they are driven from the Head. One by one, the Snarls give way, being combed or brushed down, and out, finally to slide off the end of the Hair, back into the pillows or on to the wind.

Even the Tangles flee at last, leaving the Hair smooth and shiny and beautiful looking, to be braided or put into pigtails or ponytails by the Mommies and Daddies.

But the Snarls are sly. They wait, for they know that braids work loose, and the Hair sneaks out of the pigtails or ponytails, out of the hair ties and bands and barrettes. Where ever hair is curly or long and loose and fine, the Snarls will seize their chance. For the Snarls live in pillows and on the wind, and they wait, watching, for places to build their homes.

But the Mommies and the Daddies, with their Combs and Brushes, Water and Soap and Conditioner, are waiting too. And when they see the first hint of a Tangle, the sight of a Snarl, watch out! There, out goes another Snarl! And another! Ha! Victory!

Books By Becca Price

Children have always delighted in fairy tales, tales of adventure and challenge in magical lands where dragons live and The Dark is a thing to be feared and explored. From the original Grimm's fairy tales through Andrew Lang's colorful fairy books to modern classics like Robert Munsch's The Paperbag Princess, there will always be a need for, and a place for, fairy tales. My fairy tales continues on in this tradition, with silly, serious, and poetic stories

Newsletter Signup

If you want us to let you know when Quests and Fairy Queens, other collections, or when some of our single short stories will be coming out, you can sign up for our mailing list at Newsletter Signup at http://eepurl.com/JA5e1

Dragons and Dreams: Bedtime Stories

Brave princesses, grumpy dragons, princes competing for a kingdom, and children seeking answers to age-old questions. These six modern fairy tales include stories for pleasant dreams, and stories for stirring thought. They are just the right length for bedtime reading. Each is a gem that will delight the entire family.

Fairies and Fireflies: Bedtime Stories

In the Wide, Wild Field, friendship is bigger than fear, and can be found in the unlikeliest of places.

A butterfly fairy gets a kitten, raids a beehive, and makes friends with a firefly. Urisk the brownie gets a new home, and finds help overcoming his fear of the dark. Fireflies learn that friends come in all shapes and sizes, and let you be who you really are.

This collection includes the bonus story, Sunflower, which was also published in Dragons and Dreams.

Quests and Fairy Queens

Quests are found in many guises, and Fairy Queens are not always what they seem. (coming soon)

Heart of Rock

Once upon a distant time, wizards carved hideous gargoyles, and gifted them with life with the talisman, the Heart of Rock. And once upon a time a few hundred years later, a brave cobbler sought the Heart of Rock to save his kingdom from invaders. But, without the Heart of Rock, the Gargoyles cannot live.

Two kingdoms in crisis. Two heroes. One amulet.

"Heart of Rock" is three interconnected stories that show both sides of a quest story. When one quest finds a magical amulet, what happens to the people who lose it?

"Heart of Rock" will also appear in the collection "Quests and Fairy Queens"

Child of Promise

After a summer when nothing seems to go well for a small village, the villagers are concerned that they may not survive the harsh winter. Young Agnes is chosen to go to the mountain top to seek wisdom and guidance.

This winter holiday story is not overtly religious nor sentimental, but still conveys some of the spirit of the holiday season.

This story also appears in the collection Dragons and Dreams.

The Snarls

The Snarls. They live on pillows and in the wind, just waiting to move into long, fine, or curly hair. And when they move in, they make nests, and more Snarls, and more nests. But they also have their natural enemies: a comb, a brush, and the dreaded Detangler spray!

This charming story makes hair combing of difficult hair not only enjoyable but a silly experience.

About the Author

Becca Price lives in a small town in south-eastern Michigan on ten acres of weeds, swamps, and trees. She lives with her husband, two children, and three cats.

Word-of-mouth is crucial for any author to succeed. If you enjoyed this book, please consider leaving a review at Amazon, even if it's only a line or two; it would make all the difference and would be very much appreciated.

About the Artists

Cover art was done by Victoria Clayton.

Interior art by Tanya Gleadall. Tanya is a self taught artist who especially enjoys painting people and their hobbies. To see samples of her work, visit her at tanyagleadall.com

Dedication

To my mother, Caroline Price, who gave me a love of the mythic. To my father, Clark Price, who gave me my first Kindle, and thereby unleashed a whole new world. And to Tori, whose hair inspired this story.

Made in the USA
Charleston, SC
10 April 2014